This book belongs to

_____

Published by Advance Publishers
© 1998 Disney Enterprises, Inc.
All rights reserved. Printed in the United States.
No part of this book may be reproduced or copied in any form
without the written permission of the copyright owner.

Written by Ronald Kidd
Illustrated by Adam Devaney, Dean Kleven, and Diana Wakeman
Produced by Bumpy Slide Books

The edition containing the full text of Bambi, A Life in the Woods by Felix Salten,
is published by Simon & Schuster.

ISBN: 1-57973-008-6

10 9 8 7 6 5 4 3 2 1

Walt Disney's
Bambi

A Noisy Neighbor

It was spring, and Bambi was chasing butterflies. He chased them through the trees and into the meadow, where they landed in a field of flowers.

"Hello, Bambi," said one of the flowers. Surprised, Bambi stumbled backward, landing with a PLOP on his fluffy tail.

The flower danced and wiggled, and finally a nose popped out. The nose belonged to Flower the skunk.

"Hello, Bambi," he repeated. "Want to play hide-and-seek?"

Before Bambi could answer, Thumper came hopping through the meadow.

"You're it!" he exclaimed, tagging Flower. Then he turned to Bambi and said, "Come on, let's hide!"

Bambi followed Thumper across a stream to the low hill where Thumper's family lived.

"Flower will never find us in here," said the little rabbit. "Follow me!" And with that, Thumper disappeared down a hole, forgetting Bambi was too big to fit.

Bambi tried to follow, but only got as far as his ears. A moment later, he felt a cold nose nudging his shoulder.

"You're it!" said Flower.

Just then Thumper popped out of the hole. "I'm tired of hide-and-seek," he said. "Let's do something else."

"Like what?" asked Bambi.

Thumper grinned. "We can thump — and I know just the place to do it."

Thumper led them to his favorite spot in the forest, a hollow log that was perfect for thumping. But as they drew near, the three friends heard a loud thud that echoed through the forest. It was followed by another, then another.

Peering out through the tall grass, they saw a beaver next to the hollow log. As they watched, he raised his tail and smacked the log like a drum.

Bambi and Flower watched, enjoying the concert. But Thumper wasn't pleased. He scurried into the clearing and complained, "Excuse me! That's my log!"

"And who are you?" asked the beaver.

"They call me Thumper — and here's why." He hopped onto the log and thumped it with his foot.

The beaver replied, "Glad to meet you, Thumper. I'm Edgar." With that, the beaver gave the log a good whack with his tail and disappeared among the trees.

The next day Bambi, Flower, and Thumper were romping through the woods when they spotted Edgar up ahead.

The beaver was scurrying along, collecting branches and twigs.

"Hey, what do you think you're doing?"
Thumper asked him.

"Gathering supplies," Edgar said pleasantly.

"Well," Thumper replied, "you can't just go
around taking them like that."

"Then I'll take them like this," Edgar replied.
Gripping the branches in his teeth, he walked off.

Later that afternoon Bambi, Thumper, and Flower headed down to the stream to play. As they approached, they heard a crash. Hurrying to see what had happened, they saw a tree stretched across the water. Standing next to it was — you guessed it — Edgar.

"Now what's he doing?" Thumper asked.

"I think he chopped down that tree with his teeth!" said Flower.

"He can't do that!" Thumper exclaimed. "He'll destroy the woods!"

"I know what he's doing," said Bambi. "Edgar's building a house. Beavers make their houses of sticks, logs, and mud. They're built across streams and rivers, so they also become dams. Friend Owl told me all about it."

"What's a dam?" asked Flower.

Bambi said, "It's something that blocks the water. When the water slows down, it makes a pond."

"Well, whatever it is, I don't like it," said Thumper as he stomped off into the forest. "I don't like it one bit!"

As the days passed, the dam grew bigger, and so did the pond. Bambi and Flower went there often to splash and play — but not with Thumper. He just sat by his house, grumbling and watching his friends.

Then, one rainy night, Thumper and his family were asleep inside their house, deep beneath the ground. Suddenly they were awakened by a loud thud. The others couldn't figure out what the noise was, but Thumper knew right away.

Hopping mad, Thumper hurried outside, where
he found Edgar slapping his tail on a hollow log
over and over again.

"What do you mean, waking us up like that?"
Thumper demanded.

"I was trying to warn you," said Edgar. "The rain made the pond rise, and it's almost to your door!"

Looking down, Thumper saw that Edgar was right. The pond had grown into a lake, and with every passing moment it inched farther up the hill. Thumper leapt into action. He dove into the burrow and called to his family, "The water's rising! We have to leave! Hurry!"

Within minutes he had rounded up the entire group and led them to safety on another, higher hilltop.

Bambi and Flower, who had also heard the alarm, found Edgar at the door of Thumper's house. The beaver was busy building a wall of sticks and mud to keep out the water.

"I don't think it's going to be enough," Bambi said. "The water's rising too fast."

Flower shook his head sadly. "Poor Thumper. His house will be ruined."

"Maybe not," said Edgar. "I have an idea."

Edgar jumped into the water and swam across to the dam. He began digging through it at one end, scooping out mud and chewing through sticks and bark as fast as he could.

When Bambi saw what Edgar was doing,
he raced around to the other side of the pond.
Scrambling out onto the dam, he pawed at it
with his hooves, trying to help Edgar tear a hole
through it.

Meanwhile the pond rose higher and higher.

The water was just inches from the front door of Thumper's house when Edgar and Bambi finally broke a hole in the dam. Water began to flow through it, and the pond grew smaller.

In no time at all, Thumper's house was out of danger.

Bambi and Edgar let out a sigh of relief. "We did it!" Bambi shouted.

Suddenly the dam shivered beneath him. The force of the water was making the hole wider, and Edgar realized the dam might soon come apart.

"Bambi!" cried Edgar. "Here, follow me!"

Edgar scrambled up beside Bambi, leading him away from the hole and across the dam. Bambi stumbled, but Edgar helped him to his feet, and the two of them kept on moving.

When they reached the other side, Edgar and Bambi leapt to safety. As they did, the dam broke apart in a dozen places. With a loud roar, it went washing downstream in a jumble of sticks and logs.

Bambi and Edgar joined the others on high
ground and watched the last of Edgar's house float
down the stream.

Edgar turned to Thumper and said, "I built the
dam too close to your house. Please forgive me.

I'm afraid I haven't been a very good neighbor."

"You rescued my family," said Thumper. "Then you tore down your own house to save mine. You're the best neighbor."

"I'm the one who hasn't been a good neighbor," Thumper added. "I should have welcomed you to the forest, but I didn't. And you helped me anyway. How can I ever thank you?"

"I know how," said Bambi.

The next day, Edgar began building a new house, farther downstream this time. Right there beside him were Thumper, Flower, and Bambi, collecting twigs and branches, carrying them to the stream, and helping Edgar pack them together to form a new dam.

After a few hours they stopped to take a break. When they did, Thumper hopped onto a log and began thumping it with his foot.

"It sounds good," said Thumper, "but I think something's missing."

He smiled at Edgar, who jumped up beside him and pounded the log with his tail. A loud thumping echoed through the forest. Thumper joined in, and soon the woods were filled with a happy rhythm, a neighborly beat that was part thump and part thud — part welcome and part thank-you.

Good neighbors are friendly,
Good neighbors are sweet.
They try to make friends
With the people they meet.
So if you're out playing
And see someone new,
Be sure to say welcome
And how do you do!